Peter Sís

FIRE TRUCK

Greenwillow Books, New York

Gouache paints were used to create the full-color art.
The text type is Futura Extra Black.
Copyright © 1998 by Peter Sís
www.williammorrow.com
Printed in Singapore by Tien Wah Press
First Edition   10   9   8   7   6   5   4   3   2   1

Library of Congress Cataloging-in-Publication Data

Sís, Peter
Fire truck / by Peter Sís.
p.   cm.
Summary: Matt, who loves fire trucks, wakes up one morning
to find that he has become a fire truck, with one driver, two ladders,
three hoses, and ten boots. Features a gate-fold
illustration that opens into a three-page spread.
ISBN 0-688-15878-1
1. Toy and movable books—Specimens.   [1. Fire engines—Fiction.
2. Counting.   3. Toy and movable books.]   I. Title.
PZ7.S6219Fi   1998   [E]—dc21
97-29320   CIP   AC

for
the firefighters of Ladder 20,
Fire Department,
City of New York

and
for Matej

Once there was a little boy named Matt who loved fire trucks.

His first words in the morning were "fire truck."

The last thing he said before

he went to bed was "fire truck."

And one day

when he woke up, he was

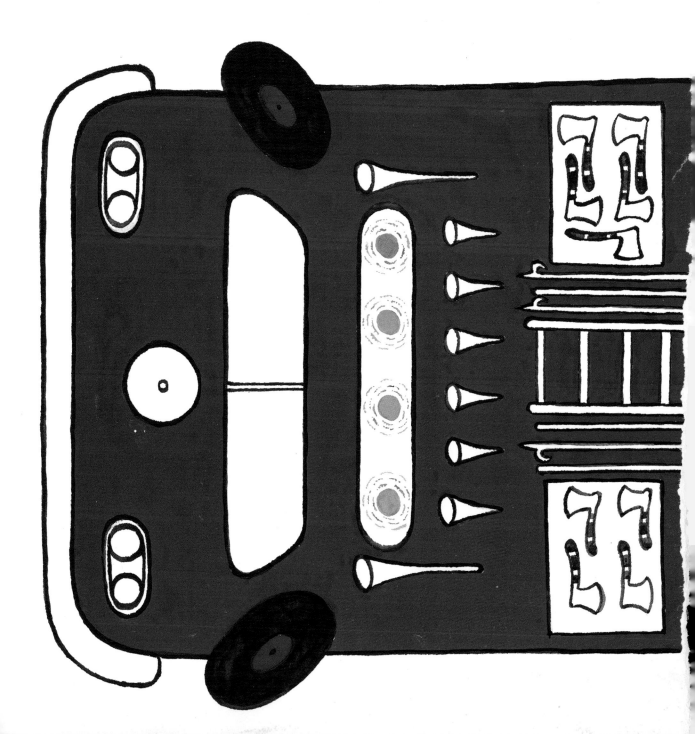

A
FIRE
TRUCK

He had

 one driver

 two ladders

 three hoses

 four flashing lights

 five helmets

 six wheels

 seven long hooks

 eight sirens

 nine axes

 ten boots

He drove around his neighborhood

with sirens blaring.

He raced down
the road.

He rescued a cat.

He put out a fire.

He saved a teddy bear.

Then he smelled something.

It was pancakes.

The fire truck parked at the kitchen table—

and Matt ate his breakfast.